Clifford's
Best Friend

The author thanks Manny Campana and Grace Maccarone
for their contributions to this book.

Copyright © 2000, 2011 by Norman Bridwell

ISBN 978-0-545-22324-9

10 9 8 7 6 5 4 3 2 1   11 12 13 14/0

Printed in the U. S. A.   40
This edition printing, September 2011

Clifford's
Best Friend

Norman Bridwell

SCHOLASTIC INC.
New York   Toronto   London   Auckland
Sydney   Mexico City   New Delhi   Hong Kong

This is Clifford's best friend.

Her name is Emily Elizabeth.

She wakes up early
in the morning.

She says hello to Clifford.

She eats breakfast.

Then she feeds Clifford breakfast.

Clifford takes Emily Elizabeth
to school.

Clifford cannot go inside school.
He stays outside.

After school, Clifford takes
some friends for a ride.

Then Emily Elizabeth does
her homework.

Now her homework is done.
Emily Elizabeth and her friends
play with their dogs.

The dogs like to play catch.
Clifford wants to play catch, too.

No, Clifford.

That is not a stick.

That is a tree.

Clifford puts the tree back.
Good dog, Clifford.

Clifford thinks he sees a big Frisbee.
He wants to catch it.

Clifford catches the Frisbee.
He puts it down.

Look! Purple aliens!
It isn't a Frisbee after all!

The aliens see Clifford.
Then they fly away fast.

Clifford and Emily Elizabeth eat dinner.

After dinner, Emily Elizabeth
gets ready for bed.

She says good night to her big red dog.

Then she dreams sweet dreams.

Emily Elizabeth loves Clifford.
He is her best friend!